Miss Nelson Is Back

MISS NELSON IS BACK

HARRY ALLARD
JAMES MARSHALL

HOUGHTON MIFFLIN COMPANY   BOSTON

For Miss Audrey Bruce

Library of Congress Cataloging in Publication Data
Allard, Harry.
        Miss Nelson is back.

        Summary: When their teacher has to go away for
a week, the kids in room 207 plan to "really act
up."
        [1. School stories.   2. Teachers—Fiction]
I. Marshall, James, 1942-   II. Title.
PZ7.A413Mh 1982   [E]   82-9357
ISBN 0-395-32956-6

Printed in the United States of America
Y   IO

One Friday Miss Nelson told her class that
she was going to have her tonsils out.
"I'll be away next week," she said.
"And I expect you to behave."
"Yes, Miss Nelson," said the kids in 207.

But at recess it was another story.

"Wow!" said the kids. "While Miss Nelson is away, we can really act up!"

"Not so fast!" said a big kid from 309.

"Haven't you ever heard of Viola Swamp?"

"Who?" said Miss Nelson's kids.

"Miss Swamp is the meanest substitute
in the whole world," said the big kid.
"Nobody acts up when she's around."
"Oooh," said Miss Nelson's kids.
"She's a real witch," said the big kid.
"Oooh," said Miss Nelson's kids.

"I'll just bet you get the Swamp!" said the big kid.

On Monday morning Miss Nelson's kids were all
in their seats.
They were very nervous.
Some of them had not slept well all weekend.

"If we get the Swamp, I'll just die," said one kid.
They heard footsteps in the hall.

Slowly the knob turned.

And the door opened . . .

It was Mr. Blandsworth, the principal.

"I shall personally take over this class," he said.

Miss Nelson's kids were *so* relieved.

But they soon learned that Mr. Blandsworth
was not a lot of fun.

All morning Mr. Blandsworth tried to amuse the class
with his corny card tricks.
"Oh, brother," said the class.

That afternoon Mr. Blandsworth showed the class
his favorite shadow pictures.
"This is kids' stuff," said the class.

The next day Mr. Blandsworth demonstrated
his favorite bird calls.
They were not a success.

And for two days Mr. Blandsworth showed slides
of his goldfish Lucille.
Miss Nelson's kids had never been so bored.

While dusting erasers in the schoolyard,
three of the ringleaders of 207 discussed the situation.
"Something will have to be done," they said.
"We must get rid of Blandsworth."

And they hatched a plot.

After school they painted and sewed
and borrowed some old clothes.

And they practiced some very difficult
stunt work in the back yard.

The next day they weren't in class.
"That's too bad," said Mr. Blandsworth.
"They'll miss all the excitement."

Mr. Blandsworth was about to show the class
his collection of ballpoint pens
from all over the world,
when someone came to the door.

Slowly the knob turned.

And the door opened . . .

"Oh, look!" said the class. "Miss Nelson is back!"

A tall and lumpy Miss Nelson tottered into the room.

Mr. Blandsworth was surprised.

"You're back sooner than we expected," he said.

The tall and lumpy Miss Nelson didn't speak.

"Er," said the kids. "Her throat must still be sore."

"Are you sure you're well enough?" said Mr. Blandsworth.

"She's sure," said the kids.

"Well, in that case," said the principal, "I'll be getting back to the office. Nice to have you back, Miss Nelson." And he left the room.

"Hot dog!" cried the class.

"We got rid of Blandsworth!

Now we can do just as we please!"

And at the stroke of ten, the kids from 207

left the building.

No one stopped them.

They went straight to the movies, where they saw
The Monster That Ate Chicago — twice.
"This is really living," they said.

Afterward they went to Lulu's, where
they stuffed themselves silly.
But soon they made a serious mistake.

Heading back to school, they passed Miss Nelson's house.

Miss Nelson couldn't believe her eyes.

"Those are my kids!" she said in a scratchy voice.

"What are they doing out of school?

And who is that with them?"

Miss Nelson telephoned
Mr. Blandsworth to see
what was going on.

"You're not Miss Nelson,"
said Blandsworth.
"Miss Nelson is back."

And he hung up.
"Can't fool me," he said.
"Hmm," said Miss Nelson.
"Something will have
to be done."
And she went to her closet.

Back in 207 Miss Nelson's kids were spending
an agreeable afternoon.

They were very pleased with themselves.
"We should do this more often," they said.
They did not notice the figure out in the hall.

Slowly the knob turned.

And the door opened . . .

"My name is Viola Swamp," said the lady in a scratchy voice.

"Yipes!" cried the kids. "The Swamp!"

"That's right!" said Miss Swamp.
"And I'm here to whip this class into shape.
Get back to those desks on the double!"

The class did as it was told.
The big kid from 309 was certainly right
—Miss Swamp was a real witch!

She knew how to get results.

The class did a whole week's work in no time.

"We shouldn't have gotten rid of Blandsworth," they said.

"Pipe down!" said the Swamp, "or..."
Just then something under a desk
attracted her attention.

It was a mask.

"Ah ha!" said Miss Swamp. "So *that's* your little game!"
And she tried on the mask—just as Mr. Blandsworth
stepped into the room.

"Miss Nelson," said Blandsworth, "I'm of the opinion that
someone has been impersonating you."

"Uh oh," whispered the kids.

"You don't say," said Miss Swamp.
"Probably just some kids acting up.
I'm *sure* it won't happen again."
And Mr. Blandsworth left.

"And it won't, will it?" said Miss Swamp to the class.

"Because the Swamp will be watching!"

A minute later, Miss Nelson appeared.

"I'm back," she said.

"Hot dog!" cried the kids. "Are we glad to see you!"

"Didn't you have fun with Mr. Blandsworth?" asked Miss Nelson.

"Er," said the kids.

They decided not to mention Miss Viola Swamp.

But they wondered why Miss Nelson hadn't seen her in the hall.